Some words
about burglars:

"Where's me cods?
Where's me 'addocks?!!"
The fish-and-chip-shop owner

"Zem clever kidskies are after us."
Olaf the Russian burglar

"You're not doing any fingerprinting
with my icing sugar!"
Gabby's mum

"Call the police if they grab me!"
Daisy's second favourite teddy bear

"NEE NOR NEE NOR!!!!"
A very loud police car

www.daisyclub

More Daisy adventures!

DAISY

and the TROUBLE with
BURGLARS

by Kes Gray

RED FOX

DAISY AND THE TROUBLE WITH BURGLARS
A RED FOX BOOK 978 1 849 41681 8

First published in Great Britain by Red Fox,
an imprint of Random House Children's Publishers UK
A Random House Group Company

This edition published 2013

3 5 7 9 10 8 6 4

The Random House Group Limited supports the Forest Stewardship Council® (FSC®),
the leading international forest-certification organisation. Our books carrying the FSC
label are printed on FSC®-certified paper. FSC is the only forest-certification scheme
supported by the leading environmental organisations, including Greenpeace. Our
paper procurement policy can be found at www.randomhouse.co.uk/environment.

MIX
Paper from
responsible sources
FSC® C016897

Set in Vag Rounded

RANDOM HOUSE CHILDREN'S PUBLISHERS UK
61–63 Uxbridge Road, London W5 5SA

www.**randomhousechildrens**.co.uk
www.**totally**random**books**.co.uk
www.**randomhouse**.co.uk

Addresses for companies within The Random House Group Limited can be found at:
www.randomhouse.co.uk/offices.htm

THE RANDOM HOUSE GROUP Limited Reg. No. 954009

A CIP catalogue record for this book is available from the British Library.

Printed and bound in Great Britain by CPI Group (UK) Ltd, Croydon, CR0 4YY

To Kathy,
best wishes on your retirement!

CHAPTER 1

The **trouble with burglars** is they are really hard to catch.

If burglars were easier to catch, then my mum would never have got told off by a policeman this evening. Or let a policeman see her in her nightie. Or had her car taken away.

Catching burglars is one of the

hardest things to do in the whole wide world. Especially if you've only got one box of icing sugar. And no fingerprinting brush. And no microscopes either. Which isn't my fault!

CHAPTER 2

I knew something exciting was happening this morning because the phone in our house rang at 6.52!

The **trouble with phone calls** is it's really hard to know what's being said unless you are one of the people who is holding the phone. Even when I sat right up close beside my mum and strained my ears really hard, I still couldn't tell what she was talking about.

Whatever was being said in the phone call was definitely, definitely, really, really interesting though. These are the words that I could hear clearly:

Aha?

Aha.

Aha.

Aha.

Aha.

Aha.

Aha.

No.

Aha.

Aha.

Aha.

Aha.

Noooo . . .

Nooooooooooo . . .

Aha.

They didn't?

Three?

In one night?

Aha.

Aha.

Aha.

Aha.

Nooooo . . . they never.

Anything valuable?

Aha.

Aha.

Aha . . .

That's terrible.

Haddock?

Haddock and cod too!

Noooo.

No.

Nooooo.

Nooooo . . .

No burglar alarm then . . . !

I bet they'll get one now.

As soon as Mum said the 'b' word,
I knew exactly what had happened.
Well, not exactly. But almost exactly.

Someone – I wasn't sure who . . .

somewhere – I wasn't sure where . . .

had . . .

for absolutely definite . . .

wait for it . . .

been burgled!

CHAPTER 3

As soon as Mum put the phone down, I jumped on her lap and asked her who she had been talking to.

The **trouble with jumping on someone's lap** is you shouldn't really do it if they are holding a cup of tea. Luckily my mum had been talking on the phone for ages, so her tea wasn't very hot. It was still a bit wet though.

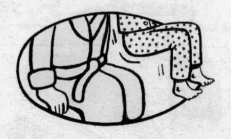

When she had dried herself, she told me that the person who had rung her before seven o'clock in the morning was Grampy! Apparently Grampy had walked to the shopping parade early that morning to collect his newspapers, and guess what? When he got to the parade, there were police cars all over the place!

Not outside the newsagent's – outside the fish-and-chip shop!

That's the **trouble with fish and chips**. Burglars can't resist them!

fish 'n Chips
NEWS
POLICE
POLICE DO NOT CROS
POLICE DO NOT
POLIC

And that's not all they can't resist!!!!!! Not only had the burglars burgled the fish-and-chip shop, they had burgled two actual houses in the same actual night too! And in the same actual town. The same actual town where me, Mum and Nanny and Grampy actually live!

As soon as I found out that two actual houses had been burgled in our actual town, I ran to the window to see if anyone had been burgled in our street too!

But there weren't any police cars to be seen. So I ran back to my mum to hear more.

Mum said that after Grampy had paid for his newspapers, he had bumped into the fish-and-chip-shop owner outside the shop. According to the fish-and-chip-shop owner, burglars had broken into his fish-and-chip shop in the middle of the night. But not only that. According to Grampy they had done it "under the cover of darkness".

The **trouble with the cover of darkness** is it covers you really darkly.

I reckon as soon as a burglar gets right under a cover of darkness, it's a bit like wearing an invisible cloak. Especially if they're wearing a black jumper too. And black trousers. And black shoes and a black mask. Black everything really.

That's what I'd wear if I was a burglar.

Grampy said he reckoned the burglars had probably broken into the fish-and-chip shop because they were trying to steal all the money in the till. Fish-and-chip shops make loads of money selling fish and chips. Especially large cods and medium skates.

What the burglars didn't know, though, is that the fish-and-chip-shop owner had emptied his till the evening before. So when the burglars tried to steal all the money, they found there wasn't any money in the till to steal!

Mum reckoned that's why they stole some big bags of frozen cods and haddocks instead.

I reckon they might have just

worked up an appetite. Especially if they had burgled two actual houses already.

When I asked what the burglars had stolen from the houses, she said Grampy didn't know. One of the houses that had been burgled was in Holly Way, though, and the other one was in Cypress Drive, which were both almost nearly quite close to where we live!

But Mum didn't know what had been taken. Probably jewels and whopping big tellies.

(Plus salt and vinegar for the burglars' fish and chips.)

CHAPTER 4

As soon as I found out that actual burglars had been doing actual burgling in the actual town where I lived, I knew exactly what I had to do. Number one: Ring Gabby. Number two: Start a detective agency FAST!!! Well, fastish.

The **trouble with starting a detective agency fast** is it gets a whole lot slower when your mum suddenly thinks of loads of other things you need to do first.

Like get dressed, have your breakfast and clean your teeth.

Mum said my detective work would be a whole lot better if I was investigating on a full stomach and without sticky-uppy hair.

When I told her that the burglars' trail would be getting cold and that I really needed to get on the case straight away, she wasn't the slightest bit interested. In fact, she even made me put my breakfast spoon and bowl in the dishwasher! And damp my hair down with a really wet flannel. I mean, what is the matter with her? Hasn't she seen actual detective programmes on the actual telly? Doesn't she know that actual detectives on the actual telly never have time to damp their hair down? Or pick their clothes and toys up off their bedroom floor?

Top detectives just get a phone call, find out there's a burglar and get on the case. FAST!

But not in our house.

Thanks to my mum. In our house, burglars get given loads of time to escape before I'm even allowed to think about starting a detective agency.

I mean, do you know what time it was when I was actually allowed to ring Gabby? Do you know what time it was when I was actually allowed to tell her that she needed to get over to my house really fast because we were soon going to be on the trail of dangerous criminals?

Twenty past eight!

Oh well, better late than never, I suppose . . .

CHAPTER 5

When I told Gabby that a house in Holly Way and another in Cypress Drive had been burgled, PLUS the fish-and-chip shop had been burgled too, she squeaked like a guinea pig! Gabby said this was easily the best start to a summer holiday we had ever had. And she was right!

When I told her we were going to catch the burglars ourselves by starting our very own detective agency, she nearly dropped the phone!

That's the **trouble with starting a detective agency**. It's exciting and dangerous at the same time.

I said it wouldn't matter how dangerous things got as long as we practised our martial arts skills in my bedroom first. Burglars are defenceless against karate chops and really good wrestling holds. Especially if you get them round the neck.

Gabby said her mum kept a pair of pink furry handcuffs in her bedroom and she would ask if we could borrow them. Then we made a list of all the other detective equipment we were going to need.

The **trouble with magnifying glasses** is no one in Gabby's family has got one and neither has my mum.

Plus no one had any bulletproof jackets we could borrow either. So we decided we wouldn't put them on our list at all.

Luckily we had all the other things we needed:

Notebooks (for doing interviews)
Pens (for taking statements)

My mum's camera (for
photographing evidence)
Orange squash (for drinking after
chasing burglars)
Crisps (for energy)
Icing sugar (for fingerprinting)

All we had to do next was meet up,
decide on a name for our detective
agency, do our combat training and
get started!

CHAPTER 6

By ten past nine, Gabby and I were both black belts in Burglar Fu (which is a bit like Kung Fu, only it's better for fighting baddies who are trying to bonk you on the head with silver candlesticks or flat-screen tellies).

By quarter past nine, the D & G
Burglar Bashing and Catching Agency
was nearly open for business!

When I told Mum that Gabby and I were starting our own detective agency and that she wasn't going to be in it, she didn't seem bothered at all.

Gabby said behaviour like that was very suspicious – if my mum carried on not wanting to chase burglars, people might think she was on the burglars' side. I said there was no way that a burglar would want my mum in her gang. For a start, she's usually in bed by ten o'clock, she'd never be able to carry a fifty-inch-screen telly by herself, she never drives above about forty-five miles an hour, plus she never wears black.

We still made her the first name on our list of suspects though.

Because we wanted to try out our pens.

After we'd made sure our notebooks and pens were working, we went through our list again and packed our crime detection bags.

The **trouble with crime detection bags** is they don't want to be too big and they don't want to be too small.

If your crime detection bag is too big, it might slow you down when you're chasing a burglar. But if it's too small, you might not be able to fill it with valuable evidence, such as burglar masks that have been thrown into bushes in a hurry, or burglar trainers that have come off in deep mud.

The best crime detection bags have two right-sized compartments: one that's just the right size for valuable evidence and one that's just the right size for all the really important crime detection things you need.

Especially icing sugar.

The **trouble with icing sugar** is mums don't like you borrowing it.

Especially if you need the whole box.

Icing sugar is the most important thing to have in your crime detection bag if you need to dust for fingerprints. Trouble is, mums just want to use it for icing cakes.

When Gabby asked to borrow the whole box of icing sugar out of her kitchen cupboard, her mum stopped her before she could even put it in her bag. Even when Gabby explained what we needed it for, her mum wouldn't let her have any. Not even a spoonful.

Or any handcuffs.

So we decided to borrow the icing sugar from my kitchen cupboard instead. Without asking my mum. That way she couldn't say no.

The **trouble with borrowing things without asking** is it helps if the person you're not asking isn't there when you decide to not ask them.

Trouble is, my mum was. She was standing in the kitchen, right in the way of the cupboard, so there was no way we could take the box out of the cupboard without her noticing.

So we needed to create a diversion.
The **trouble with diversions** is they have to be really good or your mum won't look the other way for long enough.

If your mum doesn't look away for long enough, it doesn't give you enough time to get the box of icing sugar out of the cupboard and put it in your bag without her noticing.

The **trouble with a pretend-coughing-fit diversion** is you need lots of room to do it in. Which was OK actually, because the kitchen door was open and it was a lovely sunny day outside.

It was Gabby who did the pretend coughs. Actually, they started off as coughs, but then they became more like chokes.

At first my mum just stayed by the cupboard and patted her on the back, but when I gave Gabby the secret wink, she did her

biggest ever splutter, wobbled out into the garden, fell down,

rolled over and over on the lawn, and then started panting like a hot hyena.

Which meant my mum had no choice but to run out into the garden to save her.

Gabby did a really, really good job at pretend coughing, because not only did I have time to put the whole box of icing sugar in my bag, I had time to get the camera from the drawer in the lounge, plus put some bonus scissors in my bag too! (Just in case we got tied up by burglars during our investigations and needed to cut through the ropes.)

I think my mum was quite surprised when Gabby recovered from her coughing fit so quickly. She was quite puffed out too, after carrying her back into the kitchen.

She made Gabby have a drink

of water and do about twelve really deep breaths before she would let her start playing with me again. But at 9.29 she gave Gabby the all clear.

By 9.30 the D & G Burglar Bashing and Catching Company was finally in business!

And things were going really well until about 9.31.

CHAPTER 7

I could NOT believe it when, just as Gabby and I stepped out of the front door to start our investigation, my mum shouted, "HAVE FUN, DAISY. AND DON'T GO FURTHER THAN THE END OF THE ROAD!"

Don't go further than the end of the road?!!!!!!!!!

The **trouble with not being allowed to go further than the end of the road** is it makes doing a burglar investigation almost impossible!

I mean, how can anyone do a proper burglar investigation if they're not allowed to go further than the end of the road?

Scooby Doo is allowed to go further than the end of his road. Plus that detective on the telly with the funny moustache is always, always, always going further than the end of his road. Even Gabby is allowed to go further than the end of her road!

So why not ME?

Mum said I had never been allowed to play further than the end of the road without her being with me, and if Gabby and me wanted to chase burglars, we would have to do it where she could see us. Because that way she would know we were safe.

SAFE?

Since when was chasing burglars meant to be safe!?

When I told my mum that Gabby's mum lets Gabby go loads further than the end of the road she lives in, and I should be allowed to as well, it didn't make any difference at all.

Mum said I knew the rules – if I didn't like them, we could play in my bedroom instead.

PLAY!!!!!???

We weren't meant to be *playing* at

catching burglars! We were meant to be catching them FOR REAL!

I'm telling you, I have never slammed my front door so hard.

When Gabby and me got outside on the pavement, we weren't quite sure how our investigation should begin. We had planned to walk to Holly Way and Cypress Drive to dust for fingerprints, look for tracks, search for clues, interview the people who had been burgled, write down all the things that had been stolen,

take photographs of their safes, see if their guard dogs had been given poisonous sausages, plus ask their neighbours if they'd seen or heard anything suspicious in the night, under the cover of darkness.

Trouble is, Holly Way and Cypress Drive were both further than the end of my road. So we couldn't.

Then Gabby had a brilliant idea. She said that after the burglars had done all their burgling, they might have come down my street in their getaway car! If they'd come down my street in their getaway car, then they might have left some getaway clues!

The **trouble with getaway clues** is you need really good eyesight to see them.

Especially if you haven't got a magnifying glass in your crime detection bag.

The first clue we picked up was a piece of chewed-up chewing gum.

clue 1

Gabby reckoned one of the burglars had probably been chewing it on the way home in the getaway

46

car, but all the taste had run out. So he'd thrown it out of the window.

The second clue we found was a little piece of metal. I reckoned it might have been a snipping from some wire cutters, but Gabby was sure it had come off a bullet.

clue 2

Next we found a piece of dirty paper that was definitely the corner of a ransom note.

clue 3

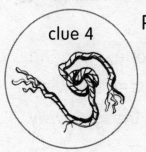

clue 4

Plus a piece of string that looked like it had come from a tying-up rope.

47

Every time we found a getaway clue, we took a photo of it and then put it into our bag.

By the kerb outside number 56 we found a half-sucked burglar's Polo mint. (Don't worry. I didn't eat it!)

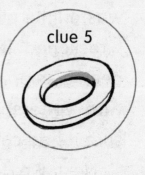

clue 5

Outside the gate of number 78 we found some suspicious leaves.

clue 6

clue 7

On the wall outside number 84 we found a burglar's glove.

And underneath an empty snail shell beneath a bush beside a wall beside the gate to number 106, we even found some dandruff that a burglar had scratched from his head!

clue 8

After about an hour of looking, we had around twenty getaway clues in our bag.

But it was at the top of my road that we found our biggest and best one!

The **trouble with skid marks** is you can't put them in your bag. Because they're stuck to the road.

The **trouble with roads** is they are really dangerous places to stand in the middle of.

Which meant taking photographs of the skid mark could be a bit tricky.

At first we thought we would only be able to take pictures from the kerb, but we were wrong. Because guess who came along on his bike, at just the right time?

Dylan!

Dylan is a really cool boy who lives in my road. He's ten, which means he's allowed to cycle much further than the end of our road without being told off.

When we told Dylan what we were doing, he said he was on the trail of the burglars too. He said everyone in the whole town was talking about the burglaries, and he had already cycled over to Holly Way and Cypress Drive to see what he could see.

Apparently the house in Holly Way had broken glass in its front door and the house in Cypress Drive had a police car outside it!

Dylan said that the policeman sitting in the car wouldn't tell him what had been stolen, but from the look on his face it was jewellery at least, possibly even gold bars.

After Dylan had used our camera to take close-up photos of the getaway skid mark, he used his special detective vision to tell us how fast the burglars had been going, how many burglars there were in the car, what car they were driving, and the first four letters of their number plate.

Gabby and I didn't know you could tell so much from the shape of a skid mark, but Dylan said that when you've been cycling as long as he has, reading skid marks becomes a real skill.

Dylan said if we let him join our crime detection agency, he could get us loads more clues from Holly Way and Cypress Drive, plus the fish-and-chip shop as well. Double plus, he would get his magnifying glass from his bedroom and let us use it in our investigations too!

Gabby and me knew that the burglars would have no chance of getting away if we had a magnifying glass, so it was decided there and then.

The D & G Burglar Bashing and Catching Agency now had an extra D!

CHAPTER 8

The **trouble with magnifying glasses** is they should really have three handles. Then three people could hold them at the same time.

Seeing burglar clues a zillion times bigger is the business!

Dylan said that the little bit of metal that Gabby had found was definitely from a bullet.

It might even have been from a bullet fired by a machine gun! But he wouldn't be able to tell without doing further investigations.

The **trouble with further investigations** is you can't just do them in the street.

So we decided we would all go back to my house to further investigate there.

When we got back, we set up a further investigation laboratory in my bedroom. Dylan said that the tiny bit of bullet metal had been fired from a Russian machine gun that had the capability to launch missiles as well. Then he said we must spread all our clues out on my bedside table, and go through them one by one to check for DNA.

The **trouble with DNA** is Gabby and I didn't know what DNA was. Until Dylan told us. According to Dylan, DNA is the most microscopicest bit of a person you can get.

It's smaller than the speckiest speck and it has the person's name written all over it.

Dylan says that you can find DNA in spit, dribble, a cough, a bit of hair, a bit of sneeze, a bit of fingernail, even a drip of sweat. All you have to do is put your clue with the DNA in it under a really powerful microscope and you can see precisely which burglar it belongs to.

The **trouble with powerful microscopes** is we only had one magnifying glass to look through.

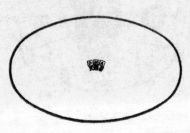

Luckily Dylan was born with magnifying eyes.

According to Dylan's magnifying eyes, our clues were swarming with DNA!

He said there was burglar dribble in the chewing gum, fingerprint juice on the ransom note, fingernail specks inside the glove, tooth marks on the Polo, hairstyle patterns in the dandruff, and struggle-sweat all over the string.

After about half an hour, Dylan finished his further investigations and told us to have our notebooks at the ready.

This is the important information he asked us to write down:

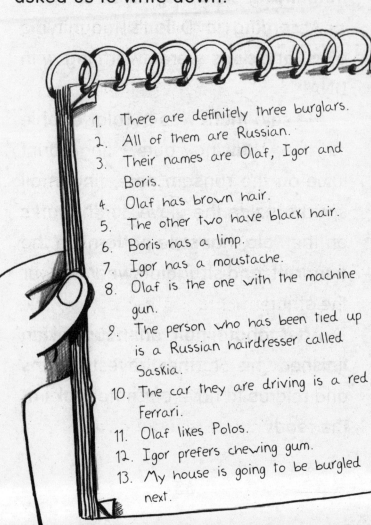

1. There are definitely three burglars.
2. All of them are Russian.
3. Their names are Olaf, Igor and Boris.
4. Olaf has brown hair.
5. The other two have black hair.
6. Boris has a limp.
7. Igor has a moustache.
8. Olaf is the one with the machine gun.
9. The person who has been tied up is a Russian hairdresser called Saskia.
10. The car they are driving is a red Ferrari.
11. Olaf likes Polos.
12. Igor prefers chewing gum.
13. My house is going to be burgled next.

The **trouble with finding out that your house is going to be burgled next** is you have to tell your mum straight away.

Trouble is, she was in the garden talking to our neighbour Mrs Pike. My mum is always talking to Mrs Pike. Even when I tugged her elbow, she didn't stop talking, talking, talking and talking. So we didn't have any choice really. We had to burglar-proof my house without asking.

CHAPTER 9

The **trouble with making your house burglar-proof** is you need SmartWater.

The **trouble with SmartWater** is Gabby and me hadn't heard of it either.

Dylan told us that SmartWater was the very latest thing in catching burglars, and that he'd seen it used by the police in loads of crime detection programmes.

Apparently, SmartWater is water that's very clever. Because not only does it make burglars very wet when it squirts on them, it covers them with stuff that won't wash off.

Even if you use a flannel it won't come off.

Even if you use soap!

The **trouble with stuff that won't wash off** is, if you're a squirted burglar, the police will always catch

you in the end. Because as soon as the police arrest you and point an ultra-violent light at you, all the SmartWater squirts show up on your clothes and your skin.

Which means you definitely did it.

So you're definitely going to go to prison.

When I told Dylan that I didn't think my mum had any SmartWater in her cupboard, he said it wouldn't matter because we could make our own; as long as we could find a bucket we could fill with water and some ingredients that wouldn't come off.

When I went back into the garden to ask if we could borrow the red bucket, my mum was still talking to Mrs Pike. And talking and talking and talking. Even when I tugged her T-shirt, she kept on talking.

Which meant I had no choice really. I had to borrow our red bucket without asking too. And some ingredients that wouldn't come off. Like:

The ink from Mum's pen

 cake colourings

Tabasco sauce

 tomato sauce

brown sauce

 shoe polish

mustard powder

 a little bit of milk

and a fish finger

Once we'd finished stirring our bucket, Dylan reckoned we hadn't just made SmartWater, we had probably made the smartest water ever invented. He said that once we had caught the burglars with it, we could probably sell our recipe to the police for loads of money and retire from school and everything.

Trouble is, it wasn't burglars that we caught. It was my mum.

CHAPTER 10

It was Dylan's idea to set burglar traps all over my house, not mine. And it was Gabby's idea to put them in my front garden too. Dylan and Gabby said that burglar-proofing my house would be brilliant fun and they were right. Trouble is, I'm not sure my mum quite agreed. When she finally came in from the garden after talking and talking and talking to Mrs Pike, she wasn't expecting to find a bucket of SmartWater balanced on top of the kitchen door.

Or trip wires in the kitchen.

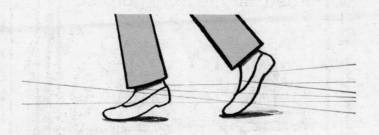

Or marbles and pickled onions on the carpet in the hallway.

Or custard and rice pudding in the flowerbeds in the front garden.

Or olive oil on the window ledges of the lounge.

When I told her that we were going to be burgled next, and we'd made our house and front garden burglar-proof, she wasn't the slightest bit grateful.

Even when I explained how SmartWater worked, and that the trip wires would double-stop any burglars from getting across our kitchen floor, and that even if they did get across our kitchen floor, they would fall over on the marbles and pickled onions in the hallway, or if they tried to climb in through a front window, the olive oil on the window ledges would make it far too slippery for them to get a grip, even in gloves, and that burglar footprints were impossible to get really good photos of when it's hot because the ground is too hard and their feet don't stick in properly – even if a burglar just came up to the front of our house and looked through the window, they'd leave really good footprints in the rice pudding or custard we'd put in the flowerbeds, because custard and rice pudding are much softer than hard ground.

I tried explaining everything!

But I think Mum was too wet to listen.

The **trouble with being too wet to listen** is it makes you really unreasonable. Especially if it's the second time you've been made wet in one day.

Mum didn't thank us for burglar-proofing the house or anything! In fact, do you know what she did? She told Gabby and Dylan that it was time for them to go home!

Can you believe that? After all the detective work and burglar-proofing we had done?!

Gabby and Dylan said they were actually thinking about going home for lunch about that time anyway, and they would leave their crime detection equipment in my bedroom for now.

Which meant that the D, G & D Burglar Bashing and Catching Agency

was now down to just one person –
me!

And all thanks to my mum.

Oh well, at least I had the
magnifying glass all to myself.

CHAPTER 11

When my mum got out of the shower, she still seemed a bit cross. She must have used a really good shower gel to wash our SmartWater off with, because I couldn't see any stains on her face or arms or anything. Mind you, I didn't get a look at her under ultra-violent light.

After she had calmed down a bit more, we had a sandwich for lunch, then she asked me to lock the kitchen door and close all the windows in the house, because we were going out.

As it was the first day of the summer holidays, I half thought she might have been taking me to the zoo, or a safari park or the seaside. Instead, it turned out we were going to the post office.

The **trouble with post offices** is they are nowhere near as exciting as zoos and seasides.

UNLESS . . .

Wait for it . . .

Unless the post office you are

going to just happens to be inside a certain newspaper shop! A certain newspaper shop that just happens to be right next door to a certain fish-and-chip shop! The same certain fish-and-chip shop that just happens to have been burgled in our actual town the actual night before!!!

As soon as I realized we would be going right up close to the actual fish-and-chip shop that had been burgled in our town, I grabbed my crime detection bag! This was my big chance not only to see an actual place that had been actually burgled by actual burglars, but also to do some actual fingerprinting too!

In the car on the way to the post office, things got even more exciting, because Mum told me what she and Mrs Pike had been talking and talking and talking about.

Apparently, at six o'clock that evening, there was going to be an emergency Crimestoppers meeting at the village hall. And everyone in the whole town was invited, including me!

Which meant if I got some really good clues from the fish-and-chip shop, I might be able to tell Dylan, Gabby and the whole town where the burglars were hiding! We might even get a reward!

When I asked my mum how many stamps she was going to be buying at the post office, she said she wasn't going to be buying stamps at all. She was going to be buying something called car tax.

Apparently car tax is the round

piece of coloured paper that you see stuck to the front of car windows. If you look carefully at the coloured circle, you can see it has a date printed on it. When you get past that date, you have to buy another car tax straight away, or you're not allowed to drive your car. You're not even allowed to park it on the road.

The **trouble with buying another car tax** is it costs a lot of money.

Mum said that her car tax had run out three weeks ago, but it had taken her all this time to save up enough to afford a new one. Plus she'd been really busy.

I said that if I got a reward for catching the burglars, I would give her all the money she needed to buy as many car taxes as she wanted.

Then I started thinking.

If my mum was driving her car but the date on her car tax said she shouldn't have been driving her car, plus when she wasn't driving it, she was parking it on the road – but if you don't have car tax, you're not meant to park your car on the road – did that mean what I thought it meant? Did that actually mean that my mum was a criminal too?

When I asked my mum if she was a criminal, she told me not to be so silly. She said she had to park her car somewhere, and in any case she had hardly driven her car at all since her car tax had run out. Plus, when she had driven her car, she had only done really short journeys. Like to the shops or to visit Nanny and Grampy.

When I said that she had driven her car to aerobics and aerobics was right on the other side of town, she started to get a bit cross with me.

Which was a bit unfair really, because *I* wasn't the one who had been driving everywhere without car tax, *she* was.

Then, when I remembered she had driven to Ikea last Sunday, and Ikea was even further away than aerobics, she stopped the car altogether and asked me if I'd like to walk to the post office instead.

The **trouble with walking to the post office** is top detectives don't walk anywhere.

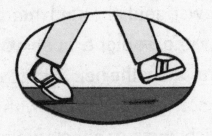

They always drive or get driven. Because they're too important.

And anyway, there wasn't much point, because guess where we were really close to now . . .

Yes, the fish-and-chip shop!

At last it was time for me to do my first fingerprinting.

CHAPTER 12

When Mum parked the car outside the newsagent's, I told her I didn't want to go into the post office and buy car tax with her. I'd rather wait in the car.

Which was a bit of a fib really, because as soon as my mum walked into the post office, I undid my seatbelt, made sure I had everything I needed in my crime detection bag, put the strap over my shoulder, jumped out of the car and got ready to go to work.

When I saw the broken window in the fish-and-chip-shop door, I nearly wet myself. A burglar had actually smashed the glass to get inside! I couldn't see the actual broken bits of glass because they had been covered up with brown sticky tape. Broken glass can be one of the most dangerous things in the world unless it's covered up.

When I saw that the fish-and-chip shop was still open, I was even more surprised! I mean, how could a fish-and-chip shop still be open if all of its cods and haddocks had been stolen? Then I remembered that fish-and-chip shops do chicken pies as well. And sausages in batter. So they probably had other things left in their cupboard that they could still sell.

The **trouble with a fish-and-chip shop being open** is it makes the door really hard to do fingerprinting experiments on.

Because every time you try and sprinkle your icing sugar over the sticky tape, people keep coming in and out.

Plus they give you really funny looks when they see what you are doing.

So after about three tries, I decided to do the big window at the front of the shop instead.

The **trouble with big windows at the front of shops** is they can use all your icing sugar up really quickly if you're not careful.

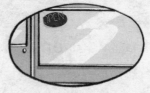

At first I tried to shake as much icing sugar as I could over the actual window, but it wouldn't stick to the glass. So I decided to do the window ledge instead.

Sprinkling icing sugar on window ledges is much better than doing it on windows, because you can get a much deeper lot on. But my icing sugar totally ran out before I was quite at the very end of the window ledge.

That's when I realized I didn't have a fingerprint brush.

The **trouble with not having a fingerprint brush** is it means you have to use your fingers to brush the fingerprint powder on instead.

The **trouble with brushing fingerprint powder on with your fingers** is it means you get your own fingerprints all over the burglars' fingerprints that you're meant to be dusting.

Luckily I had Dylan's magnifying glass to help me tell which ones were which.

I reckon I'd found about seventeen really good burglar fingerprints before I realized how many people were looking at me through the window of the fish-and-chip shop.

They weren't just looking either. They were staring and pointing.

The **trouble with people staring and pointing at you** is it puts you off when you're taking your photographs. Especially if one of the people is the owner of the shop.

I didn't know he was the owner of the shop until he actually came out of the shop and started getting cross with me.

"Why are you taking photos of my window?!" he shouted. "Is that icing sugar!? It better not be icing sugar!"

I was going to tell him that I was on the trail of the burglars, which meant I was actually doing him a favour, but before I could even begin to explain, someone else started shouting at me too.

It was my mum.

The **trouble with two people shouting at you at the same time** is you don't know which way to look first. Or which way to run.

When I saw my mum, I thought at first that she was having a hissy fit about her icing sugar. But then I saw the two police people she was pointing at.

"Get in the car, Daisy! Get in the car now!" she shouted as I raced back to the car.

"DON'T FORGET TO DO UP YOUR SEATBELT! DON'T FORGET TO DO UP YOUR SEATBELT!"

she shouted as I climbed back into my seat.

"Don't ask questions! Don't ask questions!" she shouted as we screeched away in our car.

The **trouble with someone saying everything twice** is it makes you wonder who is panicking the most.

That's when I realized that it wasn't me who had been escaping from the policemen. It was my mum! That's when I realized we were about to do a getaway of our own!

CHAPTER 13

When I asked my mum why we were doing a getaway in our car, she said it was because she didn't want the policemen to see that our car tax had run out. Which was a bit odd really, because I thought that that was why she had gone to the post office in the first place – to get some new car tax for our car!

That's when Mum told me about the queue.

The **trouble with queues in the post office** is they can be really long.

And slow.

Mum said the queue she was in was SO long and SO slow she wasn't even close to getting our new car tax when the police car pulled up outside.

Which is why she panicked.

Because if the policemen got out of their car . . .

And walked past our car . . .

And saw the round coloured tax paper on our windscreen . . .

And noticed that the date had run out . . .

Mum would get into trouble!

BIG TROUBLE!

So she panicked.

She panicked at precisely the same time that I was panicking. Which probably made us both look VERY suspicious INDEED!

Luckily we did a really good getaway! Which was actually really, really exciting.

When I looked through the back window of our car, I hoped I might see a police car chasing us with a blue light flashing and everything. Which would have been even more exciting.

But there was no one chasing us at all.

Mum said the two policemen had hopefully come to talk to the fish-and-chip-shop owner about the burglary and probably hadn't even noticed us.

Which was good because I didn't want to get told off.

But then my mum noticed her icing-sugar box.

The **trouble with mums noticing icing-sugar boxes** is when they see them, they want to know what you're doing with them.

When I told her I'd been using her icing sugar to dust for fingerprints, she nearly crashed the car. Then, when I told her that there wasn't any icing sugar left in the box, she went the colour of tomato sauce. Because it was a new box.

The **trouble with your mum going the colour of tomato sauce** is you don't think there are any worse colours your mum's face can go.

But then she went purple. Because she suddenly realized that not only had I used up all her icing sugar, I had taken it without asking in the first place, plus I hadn't stayed in the car like I'd promised. Which meant I'd stolen something as well as told fibs, on top of using up all her icing sugar.

On top of covering her with SmartWater.

On top of setting burglar traps all over the house with Dylan and Gabby.

We didn't say much more in the car after that.

CHAPTER 14

When we got home, I decided to go to my room.

Mum said it was her idea that I went upstairs to my bedroom, but it definitely wasn't. Because I'd actually already decided to go to my bedroom about two seconds before she decided that I should go to my bedroom. Which made it my decision.

Deciding to spend the afternoon on my own in my bedroom was really handy actually, because I didn't have to see Mum's face turning any other

funny colours, plus I had loads of
fingerprint photos that I needed to
investigate.

The **trouble with fingerprint photos** is they don't come out very well on my mum's camera. Because it's not a proper police camera.

Even the pictures I had taken through Dylan's magnifying glass still looked very blurry and mostly only like icing sugar. That's what happens when you don't have a proper police camera to take your photos.

Luckily I suddenly developed super magnifying detective vision just like Dylan, so not only was I able to see and draw really good pictures of all the fingerprints I had photographed, I also worked out loads of new facts about each burglar; things even Dylan couldn't see!

These are my fingerprint findings:

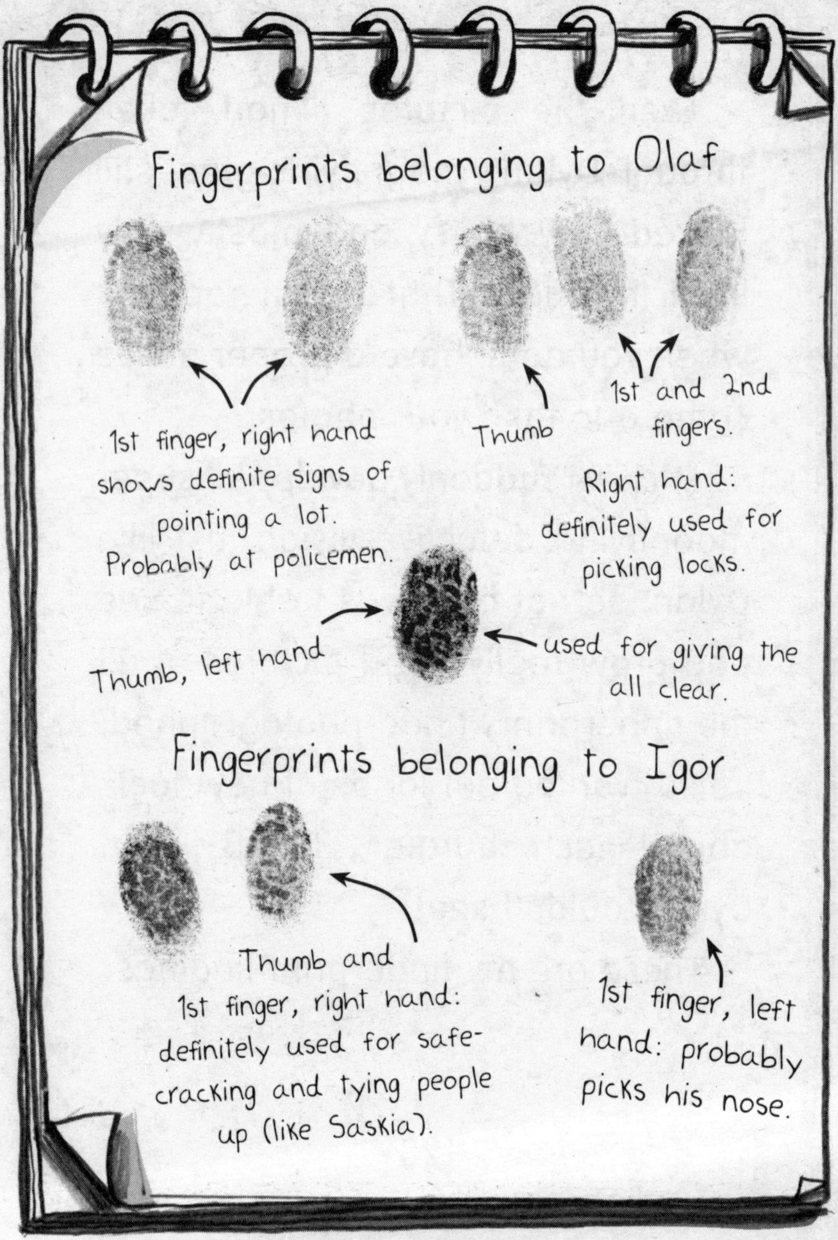
Fingerprints belonging to Olaf
1st finger, right hand shows definite signs of pointing a lot. Probably at policemen.
Thumb
1st and 2nd fingers.
Right hand: definitely used for picking locks.
Thumb, left hand
used for giving the all clear.
Fingerprints belonging to Igor
Thumb and 1st finger, right hand: definitely used for safe-cracking and tying people up (like Saskia).
1st finger, left hand: probably picks his nose.

Fingerprints belonging to Boris

good at holding
steering wheels.

2nd, 3rd and 4th fingers
right hand:

Thumbs left and right hand:

traces of filling up
with petrol.

3rd and 4th fingers
left hand:

recently unwrapped

a Polo.

By the time I had finished all my important fingerprint investigations, the D, G & D Agency was closer to catching the burglars than ever! Thanks to my icing sugar, camera and super detective magnifying vision, we now knew that:

1. Olaf wasn't just a Russian with brown hair; he was the look-out burglar in charge of making sure no one got caught.
2. Igor didn't just have a black Russian moustache; he was an expert safe-cracker too.

3. Boris wasn't just better at shaving than Igor, he ate Polos without crunching them and always drove the getaway car (probably because of his limp).

All I had to do now was meet up with Dylan and Gabby again and tell them what I'd discovered!

Plus:

1. Eat the crisps I'd put in my crime detection bag.
2. Drink my orange squash.
3. Get ready for the Crimestoppers meeting.

Oh yes, and:

4. Be allowed out of my room.

CHAPTER 15

I was finally allowed out of my room at about quarter past five. But only because I needed to eat my dinner.

When Mrs Pike knocked on our front door at 5.45, I was standing downstairs in the hallway with my crime detection bag all packed and itching to go!

But I still refused to let her in. Because she might have been a burglar in disguise.

When Mrs Pike looked at me through the letterbox and said she wasn't a burglar in disguise, I said that's exactly what a burglar in disguise would say if they were a burglar in disguise pretending not to be a burglar in disguise.

Then Mum told me not to be so silly and made me open the door, so I had to let her in. (But I still wrote down a description of her in my notebook.)

Mum said there was no way she could drive our car to a Crimestoppers meeting. Especially as it didn't have any car tax and double especially as the car park was going to be full of police cars.

When I found out that Mrs Pike would be driving us instead, I was actually quite pleased, because Mrs Pike's car has electric windows, plus it can go up to 120 miles an hour. Plus I didn't want to be arrested.

When we got to the village hall, there were absolutely loads of people queuing to get in. Mum said the queue was about ten times longer than the one in the post office! Which was quite handy actually because it gave me a chance to talk to Dylan and Gabby before the meeting began.

Dylan and Gabby were really

impressed with my fingerprint investigations. Dylan said he'd cycled back over to Holly Way after lunch, and was now certain that the burglars were armed with machine guns. Plus they had a bow and arrow that fired arrowheads dipped in sleeping gas.

When I asked him how he could tell, Gabby showed me a feather she had found in Cypress Drive.

At first I thought it was just a pigeon's feather. But Dylan said it was much more than that. He said the burglars were using pigeon feathers just like the one Gabby had found to make the feathery bits for the tops of their arrows.

He said once they had made the feathery bits for their arrows, they would dip the pointy bits in sleeping gas, point them up at the sky and

shoot them down the chimney of the house they were going to burgle.

Once the arrow stuck in the carpet, the sleeping gas would start to work.

The **trouble with sleeping gas** is it means the burglars can break into your house even if you haven't gone to bed. Because as soon as you sniff the sleeping gas you'll be asleep in about two seconds anyway. Which means you won't see or hear a thing!

Dylan said we easily had enough evidence to catch the burglars now. It was so exciting!

When we got through the doors, I found that loads of my school friends had come to the meeting with their parents too! And everyone was just as excited about the burglars as we were.

Nishta Bagwhat said her mum and dad were buying an actual burglar alarm for their house!

David Alexander said his dad had put brand-new window locks on all the downstairs windows in his house.

Paula Potts said she had hidden her favourite dolly under her pillow.

Barry Morely said he had hidden his *Star Wars* Lego under his bed.

And Colin Kettle said he had taken all the money out of his piggy bank that morning and hidden it inside his socks! (Which is why he was limping, I think.)

When I told everyone that me, Gabby and Dylan had been on the trail of the burglars all day, and that we were really close to catching them, everyone was really interested to find out more.

Except Jack Beechwhistle.

The **trouble with Jack Beechwhistle** is he thinks he knows how to catch burglars too. Except he doesn't.

Jack Beechwhistle said that if burglars tried to break into his house, they would find themselves in dead trouble. Because his dad kept a baseball bat by his bed.

Which is rubbish. Because Russians don't even play baseball.

Then Jack Beechwhistle said his dad was going to buy a wolverine for a guard dog too.

Dylan said there was no way anyone could buy a wolverine for a guard dog because pet shops don't sell them, plus wolverines are the most dangerous dogs in the world.

And Dylan should know, because he's ten.

So Jack Beechwhistle changed it to a hyena instead.

Which is rubbish as well, because hyenas live in Africa. Plus their teeth are far too wild and gnashy to be a pet.

When I asked Jack if he'd done any burglar investigations, he said he had but he wasn't going to tell us what he'd found out in case there was a reward. If there was going to be a reward, he wanted to keep it all to himself.

He wouldn't even tell us how many burglars he thought there were.

Or what the getaway driver's favourite sweet was.

I said that if he wasn't going to tell us any of his clues, we weren't going to tell him any of ours.

But he said he didn't care.

So I said we didn't care either.

Which made him stick his tongue out.

Which made me stick my tongue out.

Which made him try and look inside my crime detection bag.

Which made me push him away.

Which made him push me back.

Which made me call him a "poopy face".

Which made him call me "gorilla features".

Which made me want to arrest him.

And send him to prison for about ten years.

Without any pillows.

Or breakfast.

Or loo roll.

Honestly, Jack Beechwhistle can be so childish sometimes.

CHAPTER 16

When we got inside the hall, we sat as far away from Jack Beechwhistle as we could. Mrs Pike sat next to Mum, Mum sat next to me, I sat next to Gabby, Gabby sat next to her mum and dad, Gabby's dad sat next to Dylan, and Dylan sat next to his mum and dad. Then we changed over, because I decided it would be better if the D, G & D Agency all sat together, so Gabby's mum switched with Dylan, which meant me, Gabby and Dylan were now all in a line.

Plus it meant that D, G & D were all sitting in the right order.

At first I couldn't see very much at the Crimestoppers meeting because Barry Morely's dad suddenly came along and sat down right in front of me.

The **trouble with Barry Morely's dad** is he's really tall. But it was OK, because after I tapped him on the head with Dylan's magnifying glass, he bobbed down really low.

When his head was out of the way, I could see absolutely everything. I could see the stage, I could see a big white screen, and I could see a lady in a green dress talking into a microphone.

The **trouble with microphones** is you really need to switch them on before you start talking. Otherwise the people at the back of the hall can't hear what you are saying.

At first I don't think the lady realized her microphone wasn't switched on because her lips were moving for ages before someone at the front of the hall finally got up onto the stage and turned it on for her.

Which meant the only words we actually heard her say were "Ian Pennick".

After that, all I could hear was clapping.

The **trouble with clapping** is it makes you start clapping too. Even if you don't know why you're clapping.

Luckily a policeman walked onto the stage at the same time as we were clapping, and when he took the microphone from the lady, we worked out who he was.

"Good evening, ladies and

gentlemen," he said. "My name is Sergeant Ian Pennick. Thank you so much for attending this Crimestoppers meeting at such short notice."

As soon as he said the word "Crimestoppers", I took my crime detection notebook out of my bag and winked at Gabby and Dylan.

"What clues shall we tell him about first?" I whispered.

"Tell him the burglars are Russian," whispered Dylan.

The **trouble with telling a police sergeant that burglars are Russian** is you have to wait for him to stop talking first.

The **trouble with waiting for a police sergeant to stop talking** is he doesn't flipping stop talking at all! Especially at a Crimestoppers meeting.

First of all, he told everyone how long he'd been in the police force. Then he told us how much he knew about our town. Then he put loads of numbers and charts up on the big white screen. Then he started talking about burglaries that hadn't even happened in our town; they'd happened all over the country instead. Then he told us that the chances of us being burgled too were

Boring!

really small because the burglars had almost definitely moved on to another town and were probably doing burglaries there instead. Then he told us to padlock our sheds just in case.

Really boring

Then he showed us some more charts, and then some

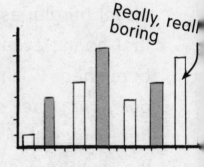

Really, really boring

more numbers, and then some pictures of cakes with different

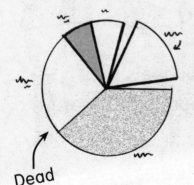

Dead boring

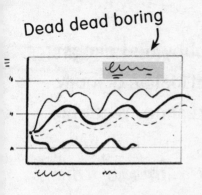

Dead dead boring

coloured slices, and then he talked about some squiggles that looked like a spider with wonky legs.

Honestly, if we'd had to buy tickets to listen to him, I'd definitely have asked for my money back.

Me, Dylan and Gabby had almost fallen asleep, when at last he actually said something interesting. What he said was this:

"The important thing, the important thing for all of us, is that every man, woman and child here today becomes the eyes and ears of the community."

The **trouble with being the eyes and ears of the community** is it's definitely a full-time job.

Because it means if your neighbours are away on holiday, you're meant to watch their houses in case they get burgled. If you see someone acting suspiciously in your street, you're meant to write down their description. Or if you see a car driving suspiciously down your road, you're meant to write down its registration number too! You have to look and listen out for absolutely everything!

Which was perfect! Because not only did me, Gabby and Dylan all have eyes and ears, we had the whole of the summer holidays to use them!

Then things got even more interesting, because once I had written down the local police station's twenty-four-hour Crime-stoppers emergency hotline telephone number (open every day of the week between the hours of two and five in the afternoon except Tuesdays or Thursdays, not including weekends), the police sergeant asked everyone in the audience if we had any questions.

At first I thought everyone would put their hand up. But they didn't! The only one that put their hand up was me!

"Did you know the burglars are Russian?" I asked.

And guess what?
He didn't!

So I put my hand up again.

"Did you know the getaway driver likes Polos?" I asked.

And guess what?
He didn't!

"Ask him if he knows what the reward is," whispered Gabby.

"Ask him if he's wearing a bulletproof vest," whispered Dylan.

"Ask him if he can tell us how many jewels have been stolen," said Gabby.

"Ask him if he's found any arrows stuck to the carpet, " said Dylan.

So I did.

And guess what?
He didn't and he wasn't and he couldn't and he hadn't!!!!

Which was a bit rubbish really, because if I'd been an actual police sergeant doing an actual police investigation using actual police cameras and actual police microscopes and actual police fingerprint powder, including actual police fingerprint brushes, I would have known the answers to everything.

After I'd asked about four more things, Mum said I should stop asking questions and let other people have a go. Which was a bit annoying really, because the **trouble with letting other people have a go** is if they're grown-ups they ask all the wrong things.

Like:

"Will you be putting more policemen on the streets?"

Or:

"Can you recommend the most reliable type of window lock?"

Or:

"Can you explain the numbers on that chart again?"

I mean, how is anyone supposed to catch a burglar asking really, really boring questions like those?

So I put my hand up again.

But my mum tried to make me put it down.

But she couldn't reach me properly.

So I kept it up.

I don't think the police sergeant wanted to hear what my next question was, but because no one else had their hand up, he had no choice. Which was good really, because my next question was a really, really, really good one. In fact, it was so good, everyone looked at me when I asked it!

"Do you think the cods and haddocks have started to thaw yet?" I asked. "Because if the cods and haddocks have started to thaw out, then they will have started to drip. And if they have started to drip, then there could be a trail of cod and haddock drips leading all the way back to the burglars' hideout!"

When the police sergeant heard my cods and haddocks question, I don't think he knew what to say. Or if he did know what to say, he certainly didn't say it. In fact, he didn't say one word at all. He just puffed his cheeks out and looked at his watch.

Which was a bit annoying.

So I put my hand up again. But this time my mum reached over and grabbed me. Except she didn't grab me, she grabbed my bag. Which meant I got away. Which gave me a chance to ask my best question of the night. A question so good that . . . guess what . . . EVERYONE clapped me when I said it!!!!!! (Except the police sergeant and the lady in the green dress.)

"Do you actually know how to catch burglars, because it doesn't sound like you do?" I said.

There were no more questions at the Crimestoppers meeting after that.

CHAPTER 17

When we got outside, everyone told me how good my questions had been. Even grown-ups! Even Jack Beechwhistle!!

On the way home, I started practising being the eyes and ears of the community. Mrs Pike told my mum that the family who lived across the road from us had actually gone on holiday to Portugal, so I was definitely going to have my eyes and ears on their house when I got home.

Being the eyes and ears of the community and sitting in Mrs Pike's car at the same time was actually quite difficult, because Mrs Pike drives much faster than Mum.

The **trouble with fast driving** is it means you need fast eyes and ears.

Eyes mostly, because the only thing my ears could hear was Mum and Mrs Pike talking and talking and talking.

The first thing I wrote down in my notebook was the registration number of a suspicious van. I'm not sure what was inside the van, but the doors at the back were tied together with extremely suspicious-looking string.

Then I saw a man with a suspicious tattoo. So I wrote down a description of him and tried to draw a picture of his tattoo. But every time Mrs Pike went round a bend, I went wrong.

Actually I didn't go wrong, my pen did. Because it wasn't a proper police pen. Proper police pens have fast ink in them that's specially designed for going around bends.

I only had a normal pen. Which was a bit of a nuisance really because I had loads of things that I needed to draw.

Everywhere I looked I saw more and more suspicious things:

By the time we got home, my notebook had almost run out of pages!

CHAPTER 18

As soon as I got in, I ran into the lounge and pushed an armchair over to the window. After all, if I was going to be the full-time eyes and ears of the community, I would need a comfy chair to sit on!

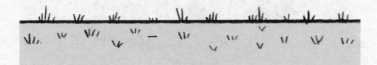

Trouble is, Mum and Mrs Pike came into the lounge just after me, with a bottle of wine and some crisps.

Then they started talking and talking and talking again!

And laughing and laughing and laughing. Which made it really hard for me to concentrate properly with either my eyes OR my ears!!

So I asked them to shhh.

The **trouble with asking my mum and Mrs Pike to shhh** is I didn't have to be a detective to know exactly what my mum was going to say next.

Especially as it had just gone eight o'clock.

"TIME FOR BED."

The **trouble with going to bed at eight o'clock in the summer** is it's FAR TOO LIGHT!

When I reminded my mum that burglars do their burgling under the cover of darkness, not the cover of lightness, she said that if I cleaned my teeth and washed my face properly, I could be the eyes and ears of the community until half past eight.

But only because she didn't have time to read me a bedtime story and because Mrs Pike was waiting for her downstairs.

So I didn't say any more about lightness and darkness after that. I put my bean bag by my window instead.

The **trouble with bean bags** is the first time you put your bottom on them, you kind of slide all over the place; especially if you've got a pen in one hand and your crime detection notebook in the other.

But after I'd wiggled my bottom around a bit and got comfortable, I had a really good view of my street from my bedroom window.

The first place I looked was the house across the road. Because if the family who lived there had gone on holiday, then this was definitely my best chance of seeing a burglar under the cover of lightness. Trouble is, there was no sign of any burglars at all. There weren't even any birds in their front garden.

So decided to look at other things instead.

The first car to drive past my house was a red one. It didn't really look that suspicious, but I wrote down its number plate in my notebook anyway – just in case it was a suspicious car disguised as a not suspicious one.

The next thing I saw was a blackbird. But it didn't look very suspicious.

Then I saw a man come out and mow his lawn. But that didn't look very suspicious either.

Then I saw a pizza being delivered further up the road, which could have looked a little bit suspicious, except I recognized the man who drove the moped because he's delivered pizzas to our house before.

The next car to drive past my house was a bit more suspicious, because it had smoke coming out of its exhaust pipe. At first I thought the smoke was probably petrol fumes, but then I realized it might be sleeping gas instead. So I wrote down the number plate of that car. Plus a description of the person who was driving it.

But after that, everything I could see with my eyes looked not very suspicious at all really.

Even when I opened my bedroom window so I could listen to the sounds outside, everything I could hear with my ears sounded not very suspicious either.

That's the **trouble with the street that I live in**: nothing very exciting ever happens in it.

MINNOW St.

CHAPTER 19

When my mum came back upstairs at 8.30, I couldn't believe half an hour had gone so quickly! My eyes and ears had only just got started! Plus it was still light outside.

When I told her that I needed more time to sit on my bean bag and watch the community and that I would go to bed when I was ready, she said I was ready for bed now.

Which wasn't the slightest bit true.

But she still drew my curtains.

And gave me a kiss.
And went downstairs.

The **trouble with Mum drawing my curtains** is it made my bedroom go really dark.

The **trouble with Mum going downstairs** is it made me feel a little bit alone.

And a little bit afraid. So I put my head under my covers.

The **trouble with putting my head under my covers** is it made things go even darker. Plus it made my imagination start imagining what would happen if the burglars came to my house for real . . . TONIGHT!

In the car on the way home from the Crimestoppers meeting, my mum had told Mrs Pike there was absolutely no way on earth that burglars would ever burgle our house, because we didn't have anything in our house that was worth stealing.

But I knew that wasn't true. I could think of loads of things that a burglar would want to steal if they came to my house FOR REAL, TONIGHT.

Like my light-up yo-yo.

And my best teddy.

And my Beyblades.

And my new colouring set.

Mum had told Mrs Pike that she could leave all the doors and windows of our house wide open all night and a burglar still wouldn't bother coming. Which wasn't true either. Plus, it suddenly made me remember . . .

The window in my bedroom was still open!

The **trouble with your bedroom window still being open** is it means burglars can get in if you don't close it.

The **trouble with closing windows when there are burglars around** is when you pull back your curtains, a burglar might be standing on a ladder outside, waiting to grab you!

The **trouble with being captured by burglars** is they will steal all your favourite toys, plus they might tie you to a chair and make you eat peas with a spoon!

So in the end I decided I would definitely have to get out of bed and close my window.

With the help of my second favourite teddy.

The **trouble with closing your bedroom window with the help of your second favourite teddy** is you still have to go with him. Because second favourite teddies can't walk. Or reach through the curtains to close a window.

The good thing though is if there is a burglar outside your window waiting to grab you, your second favourite teddy will get grabbed instead of you!

When I got to the curtains, I was almost pooing myself, I was so scared.

But luckily, when I poked my teddy's arm through the curtains and touched the window, nothing happened at all.

Even when I used teddy's paw to shut the window, nothing happened.

Which meant there can't have been any burglars hiding outside. Because if there were any burglars hiding outside they would have grabbed my teddy!

But they didn't.

So there weren't.

Which meant I had no reason to be scared at all . . .

Until I peeped out through my curtains.

When I peeped out through my curtains, I suddenly started feeling scared all over again.

Because the light outside wasn't anywhere near as light as it was before. In fact, the light outside had almost turned to dark.

So almost dark that the streetlights had come on.

Which meant the shadows had started to come out too.

Which meant that any moment now, everything outside my house would be . . . gulp . . .

Under the cover of darkness!

CHAPTER 20

After I'd run back to my bed and got right down under my covers again, I started to think even more about all the things a burglar might want to steal from my bedroom. Like my three-colour torch or my roller blades or my box of seashells!!!

The more I thought about it, the more I realized that my house was EXACTLY the kind of house a burglar would want to burgle for real, TONIGHT!

Then I had an even worse thought!

What if the burglars had gone to the Crimestoppers meeting that evening?! What if they'd disguised themselves as English people and sat right up close to me, Gabby and Dylan?

If they had, they would have seen our crime detection notebook! And our magnifying glass. Plus they would have heard me telling

Sergeant Pennick about all the clues we'd found!

If the burglars had heard about all our clues, then they would know for sure that we were on their trail!

Then I had an even worse thought!

What if they'd followed Mrs Pike's car home after the Crimestoppers meeting?

What if they knew where I lived? If they knew where I lived, they would know how to capture me, and where to steal my crime detection notebook from!

What if they were coming to steal

our notebook TONIGHT? As well as my light-up yo-yo, my best teddy, my Beyblades, my new colouring set, three-colour torch, roller blades and seashells!

I know it sounds strange, but there was only one thing I could think of to do . . .

Borrow a packet of Doritos.

CHAPTER 21

The **trouble with borrowing a packet of Doritos** is it's better not to ask first if you're meant to be in bed. Because your mum might think you want to eat them.

It's better just to creep out of bed, creep downstairs, creep into the kitchen, borrow them really quietly and then creep back upstairs to your bedroom again.

Luckily Mum and Mrs Pike were so busy talking and talking and talking, they didn't notice me creep past the lounge door. Or creep back.

It wasn't until about five past ten that Mum finally noticed they were missing. She wouldn't have noticed at all if Mrs Pike hadn't needed to go to the loo.

The **trouble with Mrs Pike needing to go to the loo** is she had to walk past my bedroom to get to it.

Which is why she started treading on all the Doritos.

The **trouble with treading on a Dorito** is it makes a really loud crunch.

The **trouble with treading on loads of Doritos** is it makes loads of really loud crunches. Plus it makes the person who's doing all the crunching go back downstairs and tell my mum.

When Mum came up the stairs and found Doritos sprinkled all over the landing carpet, she made some really loud noises of her own.

Then, when she found Doritos all over my bedroom carpet too, she went totally doolally.

When I told her that the burglars would be trying to steal my crime detection notebook tonight, and that I needed to be able to hear their crunches when they came, she said if she heard me mention burglars one more time today, she would ground me for the rest of the summer holidays.

She said that the chances of a burglar burgling our house were rarer than an egg hatching into an elephant, and there was absolutely no need or excuse whatsoever for covering our carpets with Doritos or pickled onions or marbles or trip wires or ANYTHING!

So would I please go to SLEEP!

So I said I would.

. . .

. . .

. . .

But I couldn't.

Because I couldn't stop thinking about burglars.

The **trouble with thinking about burglars** is the harder you try not to think about them, the more you do.

I was still thinking about burglars when Mrs Pike went home. Which was at about eleven o'clock!

I was still thinking about burglars when Mum turned all the downstairs lights off.

Which was at about quarter past
eleven!

The **trouble with Mum turning off all the lights downstairs** is when she did, the house got REALLY, REALLY DARK.

Darker than the cover of darkness even!

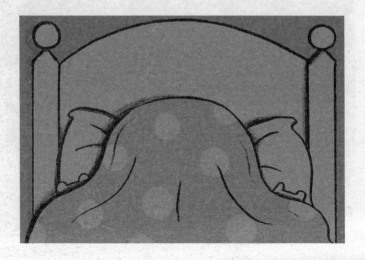

And then, when I closed my eyes really tight, it got even darker still!

When my mum came into my bedroom to check that I was asleep, I decided to make her think I was, because I didn't want to be grounded.

But I wasn't. Because no one could possibly get to sleep if they knew there were burglars around.

No one could possibly just go upstairs, go to the loo, go to the bathroom, wash their face, clean their teeth, get into bed and fall straight to sleep if they knew there were burglars around.

Except my mum!!!!

CHAPTER 22

I could not believe it when Mum started snoring!

Not just small snores either. Great big hippopotamus snores!!!

She'd only been in bed about two minutes and she was already fast asleep! I'd been in bed about three hours and I was still wide awake!

When I realized that my mum was asleep but I wasn't, the house seemed to get even darker still!

And quieter.

And shadowier.

I started to see shadows moving around in my bedroom.

Which was scary.

I started to see dark shapes over by my curtains.

Which was even scarier.

But then, just when my eyes were starting to get a bit tired, the scariest thing of all happened!

It was scarier than a shadow . . .

It was scarier than a shape . . .

It was the sound . . .

# of a creaking gate!!!

The **trouble with hearing the sound of a creaking gate at half past eleven at night** is it makes your pyjamas go all tingly.

Especially when the gate is creaking right outside your house!

At first I thought it was the gate of my house that must be opening! But then I remembered we didn't have a gate. Because it had fallen off the other day when I was swinging on it.

Which meant it must have been somebody else's gate instead!

But whose creaking gate was it? And why was it creaking open under the cover of darkness at 11.30 at night?

By the time I had crept all the way over to my bedroom curtains, I was almost trembling!

By the time I felt brave enough to peep through the curtains and look outside, I was almost shaking.

But when I looked across the road, I nearly died of shock!

Because there, in the orangy streetlight, creeping creepily around the windows of the house on the opposite side of the road, was a human shadow! Not just a human shadow either; a human shadow with an actual torch!

The **trouble with seeing a human shadow with an actual torch** is it makes you nearly poo yourself!

And run into your mum's bedroom. "Mum, MUM! WAKE UP!" I said. "There's a burglar trying to break into the house across the road!"

The **trouble with trying to wake your mum up when she's snoring like a hippopotamus** is it's really hard.

The **trouble with trying to wake your mum up when she's snoring like a dinosaur** is it's absolutely impossible.

So I had to take charge myself!

The **trouble with taking charge yourself** is at first you're not quite sure what to do.

When I ran back into my bedroom and peeped through the curtains again, I knew I had to do something, and FAST! Because the torch beam was shining all over the house across the road now.

When it turned and flashed in my direction, I closed the peephole in my curtains tight.

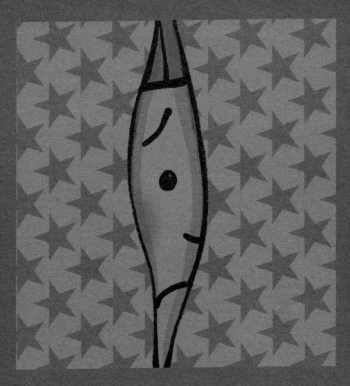

But even through the tiniest of gaps I could still see what the shadowy figure was doing. He was looking for a way to get in!

He was shining
his torch along the
downstairs window
ledges and all over

the lock on the front
door, including
the letterbox!

And the front step. And the flower pots!

I didn't know whether to gulp or gasp! I mean, an actual burglar with an actual torch was trying to work out how to break into the actual house across my actual road. Under the cover of actual darkness while I was actually watching!!!!!

There was only one thing I could do. I had to call the police right away!

The **trouble with calling the police right away** is I needed to use the house phone.

The **trouble with using the house phone** is it meant I needed to go downstairs!

On my own.

In the DARK DARK!!
UNDER THE COVER
OF DARKNESS!!

I wanted to turn the lights on, but then I realized that if the burglar saw the lights in my house go on, he would probably run away.

So I kept the lights off, did a gulp and a gasp, grabbed my first and second favourite teddies and went downstairs in the dark dark on my own.

The **trouble with ringing 999** is I've never done it before.

Which meant that as soon as the 999 lady answered, I tried to tell her everything really, really fast.

"QUICK! THERE'S A BURGLAR TRYING TO BREAK INTO THE HOUSE ACROSS THE ROAD AND HE'S ARMED WITH A TORCH AND HE MIGHT HAVE A GUN AND I THINK HE MIGHT BE RUSSIAN AND HE MIGHT HAVE A LIMP, BUT HE'S DEFINITELY GOT SHADOWS, AND IF YOU DON'T COME QUICK, HE'LL STEAL ALL THE THINGS OUT OF THE HOUSE BECAUSE THE PEOPLE WHO LIVE THERE ARE ON HOLIDAY, AND IF YOU DON'T COME AND CATCH HIM FAST, HE MIGHT BURGLE ME NEXT BECAUSE I'VE GOT LOADS OF THINGS WORTH BURGLING, PLUS MY MUM'S ASLEEP SO SHE WON'T HEAR ANYTHING IF I GET CAPTURED AND HE FORCES ME TO EAT PEAS!"

The **trouble with saying everything too fast** is the 999 lady makes you stop and take a deep, deep breath, then say everything all over again, only really slowly.

Plus, you first of all have to tell her your name and where you live, plus you need to tell her the address of the house that the burglar is burgling.

Which makes you really desperate, because if you're doing everything slowly, the burglar might be getting away!

When the police cars screeched into our road with their blue lights flashing and their sirens sirening, things got really exciting! In fact, things got so exciting, loads of people who lived in our road came out in their dressing gowns to see what was happening!

Mum didn't. She was still snoring like a dinosaur. And dribbling.

As soon as the police cars screeched to a stop outside the house across the road, about six policemen jumped out, raced through the creaky gate, and then bombed straight down the path and into the house through the open front door!

About eight and a half seconds later, six policemen dragged the burglar out of the house, through the creaky gate, and held him up under the streetlights.

That's when I closed my curtains really quickly.

Because that's when I realized

it wasn't a burglar at all.

Or even a him.

It was Mrs Pike.

With handcuffs on.

CHAPTER 23

The **trouble with people knocking on your door at twenty to twelve at night** is you really don't want to answer it.

Especially if you know that the person knocking is a policeman.

So I didn't answer it.

I pretended there was no one in.

But after about twenty-seven knocks and quite a few shouts through our letterbox, I decided that I really would have to wake my mum.

So I did.

The **trouble with throwing a glass of water over your mum's face** is it doesn't just wake her up, it makes her quite wet too.

And spluttery.

When I told her that there was someone knocking on our front door and I thought it might be a policeman, I don't think she really understood what I was saying.

Which is probably why she forgot to put on her dressing gown.

When she opened the door and found Mrs Pike standing on our doorstep, wearing proper metal handcuffs and standing next to a policeman with a very serious face, all she could do was stare.

The policeman told my mum that Mrs Pike claimed to be our neighbour and said she had been asked by the people who lived across the road to feed their cat while they were away on holiday.

Mrs Pike then said that she had had trouble finding the key with her torch, but when she had found the key and finally got into the kitchen, she had been jumped on by six police officers.

Apparently cat biscuits had gone everywhere.

Which was bad.

But then things got worse.

Because then the policeman told my mum that it was me who had rung the police in the first place.

Which meant it was me who had got Mrs Pike handcuffed. And me who had woken everyone in the street.

At first I thought Mum might be too tired to get too cross with me, but I think making her wet three times in one day might have helped to wake her up.

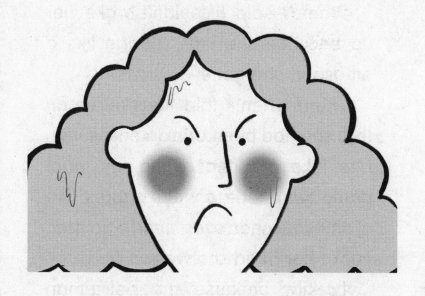

"WHY DIDN'T YOU WAKE ME EARLIER, DAISY?" she shouted. "IF YOU'D WOKEN ME UP EARLIER INSTEAD OF CALLING THE POLICE, ALL THIS SILLY BURGLAR NONSENSE COULD HAVE BEEN AVOIDED!"

When I said I couldn't wake her up because she was snoring like a dinosaur, she got even crosser!

Then, when I told the policeman that she had been drinking wine with Mrs Pike and that when my mum drinks wine she always snores like a dinosaur, her eyes nearly popped out of her head she was so cross.

Luckily, because the policeman was standing on the doorstep, she couldn't shout at me any louder. So she sent me to my room instead.

Trouble is, just as I was about to go up the stairs, another policeman walked down our garden path and

asked my mum about the car that was parked outside our house.

When the policeman told my mum that he'd noticed our car didn't have any car tax, she said she was very sorry and that she would do something about it first thing in the morning.

Then she said she hadn't been driving her car since her car tax had run out.

But I remembered that she had. So I reminded her about her trip to Ikea. And all the other places she'd been to.

I'm not sure whose face turned crossest after that – my mum's or the policeman's.

Half an hour later, our car got picked up and towed away by a special police pick-up lorry with flashing orange lights. I watched it all happen from my bean bag, before my mum came back into my bedroom and took my bean bag away.

Apparently she's going to give it to a charity shop. And if I don't start behaving myself, she's going to give me to a charity shop too.

GULP!

I've decided not to be a detective any more.

DAISY'S
TROUBLE
INDEX

The trouble with . . .

Daisy's Wordsearch

Can you find these words in the wordsearch below?

- Fish
- Chips
- Clue
- Detective
- Ransom Note
- Police

- Prison
- Crime
- Doritos
- Prints
- Handcuffs

h	s	i	f	h	k	a	e	c	s	r	m	c
n	d	k	a	c	m	r	k	l	g	k	b	h
b	l	s	b	t	c	a	t	u	a	d	h	i
d	e	t	e	c	t	i	v	e	a	b	k	p
f	c	a	m	a	c	j	m	x	e	w	i	s
d	i	a	s	o	r	g	l	t	b	e	s	x
s	l	r	t	j	w	t	o	f	g	h	o	z
t	o	t	p	h	a	n	d	c	u	f	f	s
n	p	j	r	x	m	a	t	r	r	s	l	f
i	m	a	i	o	o	b	i	i	w	t	h	j
r	b	n	s	n	s	l	l	m	o	b	e	i
p	r	n	o	g	p	a	r	e	n	a	t	b
m	a	s	n	w	l	r	j	b	b	l	h	m
r	d	c	l	e	m	s	o	t	i	r	o	d

Daisy's Burglar Quiz

1. Who rings Daisy's house to tell Daisy's mum about the first burglary?

2. The burglars couldn't steal any money from the fish and chip shop because the tills were empty. So what did they steal instead?

3. Name the two streets that were also burgled.

4. Daisy and Gabby quickly become black belts in what sort of activity?

5. What does Daisy decide to use for fingerprinting?

6. What special detective item does Daisy use to see things better?

7. Daisy believes the three burglars are from what country?

8. Two of them are named Olaf and Boris – what's the third one called?

9. What does Daisy scatter on her bedroom floor so that she'll hear any burglars?

10. Who do the police put in handcuffs at the end of the story?

Spot the Difference

There are 10 differences between the two pictures below. See if you can find them.

Daisy's Detective Checklist

What important things do you think
Daisy needs to be a detective?

Detective Facts

Did you know . . .

- One of the most famous detectives of all time was Sherlock Holmes. He was created by a writer called Sir Arthur Conan Doyle, and he had a trusty sidekick called Dr John Watson. Sherlock Holmes lived at a house in Baker Street, London.

- Another famous detective was Miss Marple, who appeared in lots of mystery books by Agatha Christie. This character has been played by twelve different actresses over the years!

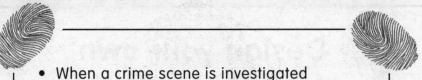

- When a crime scene is investigated for clues like fingerprints, this is called forensics. Other things that you might look for at a crime scene include footprints, hairs or threads from clothing, tyre tracks, handwriting or broken glass.

- Witnesses are very important at a crime scene. This means anyone who might have seen the crime happen, or might have spotted the criminal doing anything suspicious.

- You can test how good a witness your friends or family would be by asking them to look at a photograph of some people – for example, in a newspaper – for one minute. Then take the photograph away and ask them questions about it. How many people were in it? Who was the tallest? Was anyone wearing a hat, or jewellery? See how many things they remember correctly!

Design your own Smartwater!

Dylan helps Daisy and Gabby to make Smartwater, which will help them catch the burglars. They use any ingredients they can find that won't come off – like shoe polish, the ink from a pen, and tomato sauce.

What ingredients would you use in your own Smartwater?

_____

_____

_____

_____

_____

_____

_____

Can you remember the
first eight clues Daisy
and Gabby collected
on Daisy's street?

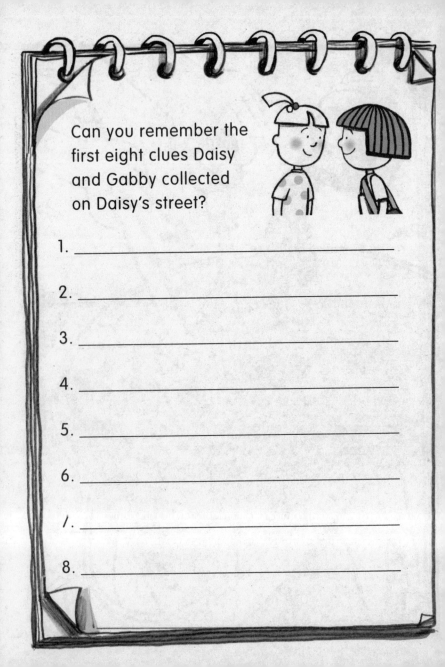

1. _____

2. _____

3. _____

4. _____

5. _____

6. _____

7. _____

8. _____

Imagine what other clues you might find on your own street!

9. _____

10. _____

11. _____

12. _____

13. _____

14. _____

15. _____

16. _____

Have you read these other books about Daisy?

DAISY and the TROUBLE with CHRISTMAS
by Kes Gray

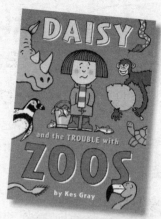

DAISY and the TROUBLE with ZOOS
by Kes Gray

DAISY and the TROUBLE with COCONUTS
by Kes Gray

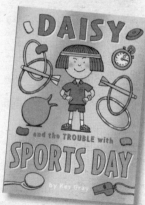

DAISY and the TROUBLE with SPORTS DAY
by Kes Gray

Answers

Daisy's Burglars Quiz:

1. Grampy
2. Some big bags of frozen cods and haddocks
3. Holly Way and Cypress Drive
4. Burglar fu
5. Icing sugar
6. Magnifying glass
7. Russia
8. Igor
9. Doritos
10. Mrs Pike

Daisy's Clues:

1. A piece of chewed-up chewing gum
2. A little piece of metal
3. A piece of dirty paper
4. A piece of string
5. A half-sucked Polo mint
6. Some suspicious leaves
7. A burglar's glove
8. Some dandruff

Daisy's Wordsearch:

h	s	i	f	h	k	a	e	c	s	r	m	c
n	d	k	a	c	m	r	k	l	g	k	b	h
b	l	s	b	t	c	a	t	u	a	d	h	i
d	e	t	e	c	t	i	v	e	a	b	k	p
f	c	a	m	a	c	j	m	x	e	w	i	s
d	i	a	s	o	r	g	l	t	b	e	s	x
s	l	r	t	j	w	t	o	t	g	h	o	z
t	o	t	p	h	a	n	d	c	u	f	f	s
n	p	j	r	x	m	a	t	r	r	s	l	f
i	m	a	j	o	o	b	i	i	w	t	h	j
r	b	n	s	n	s	l	l	m	o	b	e	i
p	r	n	o	g	p	a	r	e	n	a	t	b
m	a	s	n	w	l	r	j	b	b	l	h	m
r	d	c	l	e	m	s	o	t	i	r	o	d

Spot the Difference: